What Happens Next?

Written and illustrated by

TULL SUWANNAKIT

WALKER BOOKS
AND SUBSIDIARIES

LONDON • BOSTON • SYDNEY • AUCKLAND

"Can you tell me a story, Granny?" Little Ellie asked on the way to town one morning.

2

First published 2014 by Walker Books Ltd
87 Vauxhall Walk, London SE11 5HJ

2 4 6 8 10 9 7 5 3 1

© 2014 Tul Suwannakit

The right of Tul Suwannakit to be identified as author/illustrator of this work has been asserted
by him in accordance with the Copyright, Designs and Patents Act 1988

This book has been typeset in Aged Book

Printed in China

British Library Cataloguing in Publication Data:
a catalogue record for this book is available from the British Library

ISBN 978-1-4063-5380-8

www.walker.co.uk

For the bears who live next to my house. T. S.

"Deep in the woods, not far from here, lives Grandma Bear. Whenever Little Bear visits her, they go on an exciting trip together," Granny told Little Ellie.

"Don't bears eat berries and sleep all day?"
asked Little Ellie, curiously.

"These are no ordinary bears, but ones who wear

hats and red wellington boots, and even go on

adventures," chuckled Granny.

"So what happens next?" asked Little Ellie.

"The bears wait at the bus stop and catch the first
bus into town," said Granny.

"They go to the funfair and ride on the merry-go-round's wooden dragons," said Granny.

"What happens next?"

"Grandma Bear takes Little Bear to a shop filled with toys and lollies," said Granny.

"Before the bears head home, they stop at the park to play hide-and-seek," said Granny as she counted to ten.

When Granny opened her eyes, it was not only Little Ellie she saw: right in front of her stood a big brown ... Grandma Bear. (And Little Bear too!)

"Bears, ferocious bears!" screamed Granny.
"Don't be silly, Granny," chuckled Little Ellie.
"These are no ordinary bears, but ones who put
on hats and red wellington boots, remember?"

"Ah ... so what happens next?"

It was Granny's turn to ask.

"The bears travel through the woods, bouncing on giant mushrooms," said Little Ellie.

"Along the way, they meet Mr and Mrs Hare, a fox, a blue frog, Bob the catfish, a faun and even an ogre!" said Little Ellie.

"What happens next?"

"Grandma Bear invites everyone for a tea party of ice-cream, cakes and honey," said Little Ellie.

"What happens next?"

"Then everyone heads home and ..."
Little Ellie was feeling sleepy.

"... Grandma Bear tucks Little Bear in and kisses her good night," whispered Granny. "Good night, Little Bear."